I turned around and walked straight into . . .

Now, here's the part of the story where things start getting a little strange. I wouldn't believe me if I were you. The only reason *I* believe it is that I was there. I saw it. I don't have any choice.

I turned around and smacked straight into . . . something. This something was big and furry and black. I looked up. Peering down at me was . . . well, it looked like a cat. But this cat was standing up on its hind legs like a person, holding an umbrella in one hand, and wearing a big red tie and a tall, red-and-white-striped hat.

Please forgive me, but I totally lost it.

Published in the United States by Random House Children's Books,
a division of Random House, Inc., New York, and
simultaneously in Canada by Random House of Canada Limited, Toronto.

Furniture designed by Domestic Furniture/Roy McMakin—Seattle/LA.

www.seussville.com
www.catinthehat.com

Library of Congress Cataloging-in-Publication Data
Thomas, Jim.
Dr. Seuss' The cat in the hat / adapted by Jim Thomas. — 1st ed. p. cm.
"Based on the motion picture screenplay
written by Alec Berg & David Mandel & Jeff Schaffer."
SUMMARY: A novelization of the movie based on two books by Dr. Seuss
which feature a zany but well-meaning cat and the two children
whose lives he turns upside down.
ISBN 0-375-82470-7 (trade)
[1. Cats—Fiction. 2. Brothers and sisters—Fiction. 3. Behavior—Fiction.]
I. Title: Cat in the hat. II. Seuss, Dr. III. Cat in the hat (Motion picture).
IV. Title.
PZ7.T366955Dr 2003 [Fic]—dc21 2003002661

Printed in the United States of America 10 9 8 7 6 5 4 3 2 1
First Edition

Adapted by Jim Thomas

Based on the motion picture screenplay
written by
Alec Berg & David Mandel & Jeff Schaffer

Based on the book by Dr. Seuss

RANDOM HOUSE NEW YORK

1
The Worst Day Ever

It really was. For starters, I was sitting in the family room, staring out the window. I mean, that's *not* the way I usually spend my Saturdays.

But my Game Boy was taking a ride in my mom's purse, and the TV was tuned to C-SPAN. On a good day C-SPAN isn't exactly thrilling. Today they were covering the Taiwanese parliament, which I'm sure is plenty boring—*if you can understand the language!* The baby-sitter, Mrs. Kwan, does, and she was sleeping right through it.

To make matters worse, my allergic-to-fun, Little Miss Perfect, seven-year-old sister, Sally, was sitting right beside me.

Did I mention that it was raining?

Our dog, Nevins, was conked out on the floor. Even the *fish* looked bored. *How did I get myself into this?* I asked myself. Then I remembered. *Oh, yeah.* It had *something* to do with that little incident with the indoor stair luge.

"Ladies and gentlemen!" I'd called from the top of the family-room stairs. "Nevins! Your attention, please!"

Sally was lying on the floor, hard at work. What could a seven-year-old be hard at work on? you might ask. Coloring, perhaps?

Oh, no. Any other seven-year-old, sure, but my sister? She was studying the Fisher-Price My First PalmPilot she'd demanded for her sixth birthday.

What can I say? The girl needs help.

I heard her say, "Number ten: make tomorrow's to-do list." Then she looked up and gasped.

I admit, I must have looked pretty awesome. A shiny metal bowl was on my head. I wore couch-pillow elbow pads, popcorn-bag knee pads, and oven-mitt gloves.

"You are about to witness the third most spectacular stunt ever performed under this roof!" I announced.

Sally gave me a nasty look. "Mom told you not to mess up the house while she was gone."

"Relax," I said. "I'll put everything back." And I meant it. I really did!

I started stuffing a loaf of bread down the front of my pants—a guy's gotta protect the family jewels! But it didn't quite fit. I tore some of the bread off the loaf, stuck it in my mouth, then tried again.

Much better.

The cookie sheet was perched on the edge of the top step. I jumped aboard and rocked forward.

"Whooaaah!" I cried.

Man, was I moving! Popcorn and pillows were flying everywhere. It was great!

Then the front door opened. It was Mom! She was carrying groceries and a white dress in a dry-cleaning bag. And I was headed right for her!

I hit the bottom of the steps and crashed full speed through the bag of groceries. I landed on the wet grass and slid to a gentle stop against Mom's car.

Yes!

As I checked myself for injuries, Nevins dashed out the open door and across the front lawn. Did I mention that Nevins has a tendency to run away and that it really bothers my sister?

Bonus!

"Nevins!" called my sister. "Come back!"

I staggered to my feet. I was a muddy mess. My mom was standing in the doorway with her hands on her hips. Lying on the grass halfway between us, plastered with mud, was the white dress.

I grinned at her. "Hey, Mom," I said casually. "What's up?"

Seconds later I was back inside the house. I

watched as Mom ripped the plastic off her dress. I was in luck. The plastic had done its job. Mom's dress was untouched.

"You are so lucky you didn't ruin this dress," she said.

"Mom, I know you're angry," I said as she started wiping the mud off me. "But there's something you need to know—this was all Sally's fault."

"Save it, Conrad," said Mom. "Why today? You know what's happening today."

And I did, too. I guess I'd kind of forgotten. Or maybe I just didn't care.

For a minute I felt pretty bad. Then Sally came in with her Miss Know-it-all face. "I tried to tell him," she said. "I said, 'Mom's throwing a very important party. All of her important clients will be here.' But he went right ahead and wrecked the house and let Nevins get away. Again. I hope you're going to ground him."

"Yes, Sally," Mom said. "For a week. But that's none of your—"

"A week?" I interrupted. "Come on, Mom! Two days, and I'll give up R movies."

"You're not even supposed to be watching R movies!" Mom said.

Oops.

"I asked you to do one thing today, Conrad—keep the house clean. Do you know how frustrating it is that you always do the exact opposite of what I say?"

I was formulating a brilliant answer to this question when there was a knock at the door. It opened, and there stood our next-door neighbor, Larry Quinn. Quinn was the sleaziest, evilest neighbor a guy could have. And when you add that he'd somehow convinced my mom to date him . . .

Larry was decked out in a slick suit. In one hand he held an umbrella. In the other—

"Anyone lose a dog?" Quinn asked. He held up Nevins and walked in. "I found him next door in my yard."

My mom smiled. "Thanks, Lawrence," she said. "You are a saint."

Gimme a break.

"And here I thought you were just dating me for my good looks," Quinn said. He smiled so wide, his teeth seemed to sparkle. What a faker! I could spot it a mile away. Why couldn't my mom?

"Lucky us," I said. "Larry Quinn is here."

Quinn winked at me like we were old buddies. "Heya, sport! Call me Lawrence, okay?"

Just then Sally ran into the room. "You rescued Nevins!" she cried. "Thanks, Lawrence."

Suck-up.

Quinn turned to me. "Hey, pal. Why don't you be a sport and go finish cleaning up the living room, okay, dude?"

What planet was this guy from, anyway? "I don't have to listen to you, Larry," I said.

"Conrad, do what Lawrence says," Mom said.

I should have known she'd side with Mr. Sleaze. I retreated to the living room and got to work—work that, I'd like to point out, I would have done anyway. I can be responsible . . . when I have to be.

After replacing the couch pillows and picking up the popcorn from the floor, I started upstairs. That's when I heard them talking in the dining room.

"So have you given any more thought to what we talked about? The Wilhelm Academy?"

That was Quinn.

"You mean the Colonel Wilhelm Military Academy for Troubled Youth?"

That was my mom.

"That's the one," Quinn said. "Joan, I know you have concerns, but the Wilhelm Academy made me the successful senior VP of sales and compassionate human being you see before you."

I felt like someone had punched me in the gut. Quinn was trying to talk my mom into sending me away to military school!

2

Be Careful What You Wish For

"I'm not sure it's right for Conrad," my mom said.

"Joan, Joan . . . ," Quinn said, turning up the charm. "Gosh, I have so much respect for you. Single mother, career woman. Raising two kids on your own and still finding time to be the best darn real-estate agent in town. I know how hard it must be."

"It *is* hard," Mom said softly.

Quinn pulled out a brochure. "You have to act now," he said. "The Wilhelm Academy is what we in sales call a win-win scenario. It's a first-rate military school, and it's only eight hours away."

Eight hours away! That jerk was trying to get rid of me!

I watched my mom slowly take the brochure. Then the doorbell rang. I leaned back into the shadows as my mom and Quinn answered the door.

It was the caterer. I waited till Mom had led the guy into the kitchen, then I slipped down the steps to confront Quinn.

"I heard what you said," I sneered, getting right in Quinn's face. "You're not sending me to military school, Larry."

"Look, buddy," Quinn said. "I know I'm not your dad, and I know it's a little strange for you that your neighbor is dating your mom, but here's the thing. . . ."

Quinn glanced around. Sure we were alone, he turned back to me and gave me an icy glare.

". . . I don't like you either! And if it was up to me, you'd be in military school today!"

Just then Mom came out of the kitchen. "Lawrence, do you think you could help me bring up the extra chairs from the basement?" she asked.

"Joan, nothing would give me more pleasure," Quinn said. "But I should be on my way. I've got a big sales meeting downtown."

He wasn't fooling me. Big sales meeting, my foot. He was getting out of the manual labor!

Quinn gave me a little salute, then swept out the door.

Vermin! I thought. I turned to my mom. "Mom, that guy is a total phony. You can't let Larry—"

"It's Lawrence, Conrad," my mom said.

I was about to try again when the caterer came out of the kitchen with a tray of hors d'oeuvres.

"Good job," Sally said, following him out. "Now I've got some room to make cupcakes."

"Cupcakes?" my mom said. "No, honey, not today. The party."

Mom grabbed the hors d'oeuvres tray and headed back into the kitchen. Sally and I followed her.

"Mom, you've got to listen to me!" I said. "As soon as you left—"

"Quiet!" Mom said.

Sally held up her PalmPilot. "Two weeks ago you said today was good. *Ergo,* I scheduled it. See?"

"Quiet!" Mom said again.

The phone rang. "I said *quiet!*" she screamed. She took a deep breath and answered the phone. In her super-sweet business voice she said, "Joan Walden Real Estate! Be it ever so humble, there's no place like Joan."

She listened for a moment, then said, "Why, hello, Mr. Filene. I'm looking forward to meeting you next week. . . . Today? Oh . . . No, that's no problem. I'll be there. No problem at all."

She hung up and banged her head against the cupboard in frustration.

No problem at all, I thought, feeling sorry for her. *Right.*

"What's going on, Mommy?" Sally asked.

"I have a very important client, Mr. Filene, in

town for one day, and I have to show him some houses."

Mom stood up straighter, suddenly nervous. "I hope Mrs. Kwan can baby-sit today."

"Not Mrs. Kwan!" I said.

Thirty minutes later, Mrs. Kwan showed up, and Mom got ready to go. I'm not sure why, but I chose that moment to take out my Game Boy. Not a good idea.

"Okay, Mrs. Kwan," Mom said. "I'll be back in a couple of hours. Conrad's grounded, so no video games—"

As she passed, Mom grabbed the Game Boy out of my hands and slipped it into her purse.

"Sally, last chance if you want to make cupcakes," she said to my sister. "I can take you to your friend Ginny's house."

"Ginny's not my friend anymore," Sally said. "Last time we made cupcakes, she wanted to be the head chef. *I'm* the head chef!"

"What about Denise, then?" Mom asked.

"She talked back to me," Sally said, "so I ordered her not to speak to me anymore."

"What about Ellen?" Mom asked.

"She's too bossy," Sally said.

Mom rolled her eyes. "And you don't like bossy?"

I grinned. My sister was bossy times ten!

"I won't tolerate it," Sally said.

"Right," Mom said. "Well, if you're both staying, remember the rules: Conrad, no playing ball in the house. No fighting. No answering the phone 'City Morgue.' No telling the dumb Schweitzer kid down the street he's a robot. No telling him that robots are impervious to flame.

"And, Conrad, remember," Mom continued. "The party is tonight at eight, so absolutely no touching the food in the kitchen, no leaving your toys out, and absolutely no one sets foot in the living room, or else."

"Or else what?" I asked, frustrated. "You're going to do what Larry said and send me to military school?"

Mom blushed. "Maybe if you'd just behave," she said, "I wouldn't have to consider military school. I wish I could trust you."

Ouch! Score one for Mom.

"Well, I wish I had a different mom!" I lashed back.

"Sometimes I wish the same thing!" she yelled. She stormed out and slammed the door shut behind her.

I went to the window. My mom was backing out of the driveway. Next door, Quinn was getting into his car, a sporty Thunderbird. My mom waved at him, and he blew her a kiss. Quinn watched my mom drive down the road. As soon as she'd turned the corner, he loosened his tie and headed back into the house.

So much for his big meeting, I thought.

Meanwhile, Mrs. Kwan had sat down on the couch and picked up the TV remote.

"Children, would you like to watch television with me?" she asked us. "We don't have to tell your mother."

Sally and I looked at each other in surprise. Go, Mrs. Kwan! If only she'd wanted to watch something other than . . .

"Taiwanese parliament?" Sally and I said in disbelief. This was worse than no TV at all!

After a while, Mrs. Kwan fell asleep. Sally and I pulled two chairs over to the window and sat down. There was nothing better to do than stare outside. A butterfly flitted around the window. We watched it until a big raindrop fell onto it and knocked it down. Thunder rumbled, and it started to pour.

So there we were, in front of the windows in the family room. I slumped in my chair. I couldn't stand it! I wished that something—*anything*—would happen!

Outside, the wind seemed to change direction. For a moment the clouds spun.

Weird, I thought. *Maybe we'll get a tornado! That would be exciting!*

But whatever it was, it didn't happen again. In desperation I started tapping the fishbowl.

"Quit bothering the fish!" Sally said.

"Fine," I said. I licked my hand. "Spit hand!"

I lunged at my sister.

"Gross!" Sally screamed. She swatted at my hand. "Get away!"

Suddenly there was a bump from upstairs. We froze.

"What was that?" Sally asked.

Nevins was staring up the steps, growling. I looked at Sally with wide eyes. Someone was in the house!

3

A Very Large Cat in a Very Strange Hat

Leaving Mrs. Kwan snoring on the couch, Sally, Nevins, and I crept up the stairs.

"I think it came from the closet," I whispered.

We tiptoed over. I took hold of the handle and jerked open the door.

Nothing. Just clothes and junk. Then I had a brilliant idea.

I leaned in, then threw myself into the closet as if someone had grabbed me!

"Conrad?" Sally called. She sounded afraid. I grinned and grabbed an old teddy bear I found in the pile.

The clothes rustled as Sally poked her way in.

I held up the bear and thrust it through all the junk, right at her.

"Yaaaah!" Sally screamed.

I jumped out and started cracking up. "You should have seen the look on your face," I said. "It was like you just saw a monster."

I turned around and ran smack into . . .

Now, here's the part of the story where things start getting a little strange. I wouldn't believe me if I were you. The only reason *I* believe it is that I was there. I saw it. I don't have any choice.

I turned around and smacked straight into . . . something. This something was big and furry and black. I looked up. Peering down at me was . . . well, it looked like a cat. But this cat was standing up on its hind legs like a person, holding an umbrella in one hand, and wearing a big red tie and a tall, red-and-white-striped hat.

"A monster?" the big cat asked. "Where?!?"

Please forgive me, but I totally lost it.

"Aiiighhhhhhhhhh!!!"

Sally and I turned around, hightailed it back

downstairs, and dove into the coat closet.

We huddled together in the darkness. "What was that?" Sally asked.

"I don't know," I said. "It looked like a humongous cat."

"'Humongous'?" said a voice right behind me. It was the cat!

"I prefer the term 'big-boned' or 'jolly,'" it said. "By the way, you could lose a few pounds yourself, tubby. Now, what are we hiding from?"

This was too freaky. Sally and I burst out of the closet, ran up the stairs, zipped into our parents' bedroom, and slid under the bed.

"That *was* a giant cat!" Sally said.

I shook my head. "But that's impossible. Isn't it?"

"It's entirely impossible," someone said. The cat was right next to us again! "Scream and run!" the cat yelled.

We sprang out from under the bed and backed toward the doorway.

"Who—who are you?" Sally asked.

I heard something behind us and spun around. Somehow the cat had gotten out from under the bed to the doorway.

The cat swept his hat from his head and bowed. "Why, I'm the Cat in the Hat! There's no doubt about that. I'm a super-fundiferous feline who came here to make sure that you're . . . mee-line? . . . keylime? . . . turpentine?"

The Cat sighed with frustration. "I'm not good with rhyming," he said. "Look, I'm a cat that can talk. That should be enough for you people."

The Cat turned on his heel . . . paw? . . . and started down the hall. We followed him.

"Where did you come from?" Sally asked.

"My place," said the Cat. "Where do you think?"

"No," I said. "How did you get here?"

"I drove. You know," said the Cat thoughtfully, "I've been here two whole minutes, and no one's offered me a drink."

"Sorry, Mr. Cat," Sally said, going into suck-up mode. "Would you like some milk?"

"Milk?" The Cat shook his head. "No. Lactose-intolerant. Gums up the works. You'll thank me later."

The Cat paused at the top of the steps, grabbed a tray from a nearby table, and . . . surfed down the steps!

Sally and I hurried down after him.

The Cat wandered into the dining room and paused in front of a painting of a bowl of fruit. He stuck his umbrella *into* the painting and speared an apple. He grabbed the apple and took a bite, then tossed it back into the painting. Now the apple in the painting had a bite taken out of it!

The Cat sauntered into the family room and looked around, nodding. "Yes, this place will do quite nicely," he said. He frowned at the window. "Although those drapes are a train wreck."

The Cat walked around the couch and sat down. "And this is the lumpiest couch I've ever sat on."

Sally and I peered over the back of the couch.

The Cat was sitting on Mrs. Kwan! She snored on, completely oblivious.

"Who is this dreadfully uncomfortable woman?" the Cat asked.

"That's our baby-sitter," Sally whispered.

"Baby-sitter?" the Cat asked, surprised. He produced a coat hanger out of nowhere, stuck it into the shoulders of Mrs. Kwan's sweater, then lifted her up.

"You don't really need one of these, do you?" the Cat asked. He carried Mrs. Kwan over to the closet, hung her up, and shut the door.

So much for Mrs. Kwan! This Cat was weird, but I was starting to like him!

I hadn't seen anything yet. . . .

"Now," the Cat said, "let's have a look at you two."

We watched, stunned, as a doctor's lamp popped out of the Cat's hat. He shined it at Sally and moved a finger back and forth in front of her face. "Follow my finger," he said. "Up here. Down here."

He peered down her throat. “Hmmm . . . I see,” he said. “You’re too bossy.

“Now you,” the Cat said, turning to me. He poked me and prodded me. He even checked my gums!

“Uh-huh. Uh-huh,” the Cat said. “Looks like someone is allergic to rules.”

The Cat worked my elbow back and forth.

“Resist my hand,” he said. I pushed against his paw.

The Cat nodded. “And it appears that your mom is dating a guy named . . .”

The Cat peered in my ear. “. . . Larry.”

The Cat stood up. “Now let’s see what the old phunometer has to say.”

Out of nowhere the Cat pulled a crazy-looking stethoscope-like thing with a dial attached. He held it up next to Sally. The needle swung all the way to one side and stuck on the words SERIAL ARSONIST.

The Cat looked alarmed. He tapped the meter. The needle unstuck and swung back to CON-

TROL FREAK. It let out a dull, low-pitched sound.

Then the Cat held the phunometer up to me. The needle shot to the other side of the meter and landed on RULE BREAKER. The phunometer emitted a zany, high-pitched sound.

The Cat put away the phunometer. "Well, just as I suspected," he said. "You guys are both out of whack. A control freak and a rule breaker."

"So what do we do?" I asked.

"Well, there are two treatments I'd recommend," the Cat said. "One is a painful series of shots injected into the abdomen and kneecaps. The other involves a musical number."

The Cat tilted back his head and sang a scale. "Me me me me me me me meeeeooowww."

Sally and I grimaced at each other. The shots might actually be the less painful choice.

"How many shots?" Sally asked.

The Cat pretended to be amused. "How many shots. Aren't you precious."

He turned and called, "Maestro!"

Sally and I heard a few bars of quiet piano music. The Cat struck a pose and said:

"I know it is wet
And the sun is not sunny.
But we can have
Lots of good fun that is funny!"

Then the music really kicked in, and the Cat launched into song:

"It's fun to have fun
But you have to know how.
I know lots of good tricks
And I'll—"

"Stop this right now!" someone called.

The music died. We all looked around, trying to find who'd spoken. But no one was there!

"Who said that?" I called out.

"Me, you hairless monkeys!"

We turned around. It was the fish!

4 Rules Are for Fools

The Fish was leaning out of his bowl, glaring at us.

"The fish is talking!" Sally said in disbelief.

For once, Sally and I felt exactly the same way. I mean, how weird was this day going to get?

"Listen to me, children," the Fish said. "This cat should not be here. He should not be about. He should not be here when your mother is out."

"C'mon, kids," said the Cat. "You gonna listen to him? He drinks where he pees."

The Fish looked shocked and offended. "I'll ask you, sir, not to use that kind of language around Diver Dan," he said. "He's very sensitive."

The Fish turned to a plastic diver floating in the bowl and put his fins over its ears.

The music kicked in again, this time a much peppier song than before, with clacking castanets. Sally and I turned to find the Cat standing at the top of the stairs. He was dressed in a Carmen Miranda outfit, complete with lipstick and a dress. His hat had turned into a stack of fruit.

The Cat started down the stairs, singing right to me.

"There was this cat I knew
Back home where I was bred.
He never listened to a single thing
His mother said.
He never used a litter box,
He'd make a mess in the halls.
That's why they sent him to a vet
Who snipped off both his—"

The music skipped and jumped right to the chorus.

"Boy, that wasn't
Fun, fun, fun.
He never learned you can have
Fun, fun, fun.
Less is more.
They may ship you off to school,
So rein it in a little.
We can't spell *fun*
Without *U* in the middle!"

Now the Cat was juggling building blocks with *F, U,* and *N* on them. He tossed away the *F* and *N* blocks, leaving the *U* block hovering in front of him.

Back in his bowl, the Fish was swimming around crazily and trying to get our attention. "Children, this Cat is currently in violation of seventeen of your mother's rules."

The phone rang, and the Cat answered it. "Hello, City Morgue? We deliver!" he said.

"Eighteen!" the Fish cried. "This Cat must go!"

The Cat had disappeared again. Then he came through the kitchen's sliding doors dressed as a matador! He swirled his red cape and bowed. Behind him, Sally and I could see an angry bull. It snorted and pawed the carpet. Then suddenly, it was charging!

The Cat slid the kitchen doors closed just in the nick of time. There was a resounding crash as the bull slammed into the doors. Its horns stuck all the way through to our side. The Cat hung his cape on one of them. He turned to Sally and sang:

"There was this high-strung cat
who thought she knew it all."

The Cat reached out with his tail and plucked Sally's PalmPilot right out of her hands. Then he grabbed his cape from the horn and snapped it out. Sally put her head down and charged through it like a bull in a desperate attempt to get her PalmPilot back.

The Cat kept singing:

"The way she scheduled out her day
Could drive you up a wall.
She liked to be the teacher's pet,
Always the head of the class.
It took a ton of TNT
To kill the bug up her—"

Once again the music skipped right to the chorus.

"Ask me, was she
Fun, fun, fun?
Not a chance.
You can't have fun, fun, fun,
You're too uptight.
Lose the dictionary, kid,
Life isn't such a riddle.
We can't spell *fun*
Without *U* in the middle!"

The Cat twirled his cape into the word *FUN,* and then twirled it again into a *U.*

The music switched into a dance beat. The Cat

walked behind the TV—and actually appeared *on* TV! It was still the Taiwanese parliament.

Sally and I looked at each other. We couldn't believe it!

The Cat jumped back out of the TV and started dancing around the room again. He sang:

"You can juggle work and play,
But you have to know the way.
You can keep afloat a wish,
Like the way I do this fish!"

The Cat picked up the fishbowl. The Fish spluttered angrily as the Cat sang on:

"You can be a happy fella.
Someone throw me that umbrella!"

I grabbed the Cat's umbrella and threw it to him.

"And that fan
And that toy man,
That rake, that cake. . . ."

As the Cat called out for things, they suddenly appeared around the room. Sally and I grabbed them and threw them to the Cat, who caught them and balanced them all on the umbrella! We were having a blast! This sure beat staring out the window.

"Life's what you make it," the Cat sang, "so have . . ."

A large rubber ball appeared, and the Cat jumped aboard it, balancing himself and the stack of everything we'd thrown him. Then the members of the Taiwanese parliament stepped out of the TV!

". . . Fun, fun, fun!" sang the Cat. "No more rain. Look, it's the sun, sun, sun!"

Teetering precariously on the rubber ball and balancing the fan, an action figure, a rake, and a cake all on top of his umbrella, the Cat grabbed the drapes and pulled them open. Sally and I gasped. The rain had stopped, and the sun was out! A rainbow arced across the sky. The Cat was still singing:

"So stick with me,
I'm as happy as a clam.
Yes, I am fit as a fiddle.
Life ain't always just about you. . . ."

With his free hand, the Cat took a sip of milk.

". . . And the purebred cats may doubt you."

The Cat suddenly looked a little sick. "Milk," he muttered to us. "Big mistake."

He went back to his song:

"But remember this,
You can't have fun without *U*—"

The Cat broke off as he swelled up and let out a huge burp! He went flying through the air. Sally and I watched in horror as everything he'd been juggling went flying, too!

"I knew that milk would come back to haunt me," the Cat muttered. Then he flew into action! His hands were a blur as they shot every which way to catch things. His leg stretched all the way across the room to catch the milk saucer. He used his tongue, his ear, and his mouth. Even the hat caught a dish! He saved everything except the Fish, who landed in the teakettle.

Everything under control, the Cat stood tall and hit the final note of his song:

"... In the middle!"

The Fish poked out of the teakettle spout and started clapping sarcastically. "Bravo, Cat!" he said, his voice dripping with derision. "I think these children are smart enough not to fall for your soulless MTV-style flash at the expense of content and moral values."

The Fish and the Cat turned to us expectantly. I hated to prove the Fish wrong, but . . .

"That was wicked cool!" I said.

"Do it again!" Sally cried.

The Cat grinned. "I'd love to," he said. "But Shamu is right. I really should be going."

What?!? Just when things were starting to get interesting!

"No! Don't go!" I cried.

"All right, I'll stay," the Cat said.

"Yeah!" Sally and I cheered.

The Cat did a crazy little dance. "Oh, yeah! But if I'm going to stay, then there's something I want to show you. Something magical and full of wonder."

Suddenly the Cat was deadly serious. "It's called a contract."

The Cat whipped out a stack of paper. Each page was jammed with tiny writing.

"You want us to sign this?" I asked.

"It's just a formality, really," the Cat said.

A group of men appeared behind the Cat. Each of them was bald and wore a gray business suit and wire-rimmed glasses.

"Who are they?" I asked.

"Magical time-traveling elves!" the Cat said.

Sally and I looked doubtful.

"Okay, they're my lawyers," the Cat admitted. "Basically, this contract guarantees that you can have all the fun you want and nothing bad's going to happen."

The Cat produced a pen from his hat and held it out to us.

"All the fun we want?" I asked incredulously.

The Cat glanced at his lawyers. They nodded.

"A-yup," said the Cat.

"Nothing bad will happen?" Sally asked.

The lawyers shook their heads.

"A-nope," said the Cat.

I took the pen eagerly, ready to sign, but Sally didn't look convinced.

"C'mon, Sally," I said. "For once in your life try something spontaneous."

Sally huffed. "It goes against my better instincts, but . . . fine."

"Beautiful!" the Cat crowed.

When we'd finished signing, the Cat folded up the forms and turned the stripes of his hat like the dial of a combination lock. The top of the hat popped open like a safe, and he put the papers inside. Then he closed the top and spun the stripes, locking it.

"All righty! Give me five!" the Cat cried. Then he paused and looked at his hand. He only had four fingers. "Four!"

The three of us high-foured.

"Now come on, kids," the Cat said. "Let's get our swerve on! The sky's the limit, legally speaking."

The Cat turned to wink at his lawyers. When he turned back around, he screamed!

"A monster!" he cried, and jumped into Sally's arms.

Sally and I turned. Nevins had sauntered into the room.

"He's a monster!" the Cat babbled. "A furry monster. He's gonna murderlize me!"

"It's just Nevins," I said incredulously. "He's part Chihuahua."

Nevins had no idea what was going on. After a second, he turned and wandered off.

"He's lucky he's part Chihuahua," the Cat

said, acting tough. He looked disdainfully at Sally. "Get off me."

Sally dropped him.

The Cat got up and dusted himself off, then started looking around the house again. We followed him . . . until he went into the living room!

"Hey, check out this room," the Cat said, wandering in. He stopped when he realized we weren't with him. "Where'd you go?"

He turned. We were standing in the doorway. It was as if there were an invisible force field stopping us from taking another step.

"Mom says we're not allowed in the living room today, or else," Sally explained.

"Why?" asked the Cat. "It seems like the nicest room in the house."

"She's worried that we'll mess up the couches by jumping on them or something," I said.

The Cat went over to the couch and pressed down on the cushions.

"And she's right," the Cat said. "You can't

jump on these. Not like this. They need some adjustment."

Before our eyes the Cat's hat transformed into a dirty, red-and-white-striped baseball cap. He slapped a name tag on his chest that read *CAT* and put an oily rag in his back pocket.

"Let's have a look under the hood," he said.

The Cat reached under the couch and tugged on something, and one of the cushions popped up like the hood of a car. The Cat reached in and pulled out a jack. Then he jacked up the couch and used my skateboard to roll underneath it. Sally and I heard all sorts of ratcheting noises and the sound of an electric drill. Then the Cat rolled back out and lowered the couch.

"That oughta do it," the Cat said.

Suddenly no longer dressed as an auto mechanic, the Cat jumped onto the couch. BOING! It was super-springy! Sally and I watched in disbelief as the Cat executed all sorts of fantastic flips and spins.

"Kids, I could use a little company," the Cat

said. “C’mon, you know you want to.”

Sally and I were dying. It looked like so much fun! Finally I couldn’t resist any longer. I took a step into the living room.

Sally gasped. “What about Mom’s party?”

“What about it?” I asked, suddenly remembering something. “We signed the contract.”

So we could do whatever we wanted, and nothing bad would happen!

“Wahoo!” I cried. I ran all the way into the living room and joined the Cat on the couch. It was incredible! I was bouncing so high, I could touch the ceiling!

“One cushion left, Sally,” the Cat said.

“She’ll never do it,” I said. “She doesn’t know how to have fun.”

The Fish hopped over in his teakettle. “Sally, be strong!” he said. “You don’t need to bounce around like a monkey to have fun! We could do arts and crafts or read quietly to ourselves. . . . Sally?”

The Fish looked up, but Sally was gone!

“Ayiiiiii!” she cried, running into the living room and jumping onto the couch. We were flying all over the place!

“This is amazing!” I cried.

“It’s like being in the circus!” Sally said.

“And the best thing,” I said, “is that no one will ever—”

Suddenly the front door crashed open. It was Quinn!

5
Recipe for Disaster

"—know," I finished lamely.

"Judas Priest!" yelled Quinn, stepping through the door. "I can't believe what I'm seeing!"

Now that my mom wasn't around for him to impress, Quinn had left his suit at home. He was wearing a tank-top T-shirt and baggy, animal-print weight-lifter pants.

For a moment, I was worried about how we'd explain the Cat. But I glanced around, and the Cat had disappeared!

"Oh, Mr. Quinn," Sally said sweetly. "I was just telling Conrad to get off the couch. Bad, Conrad! Bad!"

I looked at my sister, shocked. The little rat!

Quinn shut the front door and gave Sally a smile. "Sally, sweetheart, princess, I'm going to let you in on a little secret." Quinn's smile vanished. "Nobody likes a suck-up."

Quinn grinned at Sally, then headed down the hall to the kitchen.

I felt a tap on my shoulder and turned, but no one was there. Then I saw a furry black tail tap Sally's shoulder. It was hanging down from the ceiling. We both looked up. The Cat was clinging to the ceiling by his claws!

Before I could say anything, Quinn walked back into the room carrying a six-pack of beer, a sandwich, and the loaf of bread that I'd had down my pants earlier!

Quinn took a bite of the sandwich. "Good bread," he said.

Trying to distract Quinn so he wouldn't see the Cat, Sally and I jumped off the couch and walked around Quinn. Now his back was to the couch—and the Cat.

"I thought you had a big meeting," I said to him accusingly. "Who's it with, the noon *SportsCenter*?"

Quinn snarled at me. "Put a sock in it, Billy Crystal," he said. "I know you kids are up to something. And when I find out what it is, it's military school for you, Conrad."

"Like Mom's going to listen to you," I said.

"Oh, yes, she is," Quinn said. "And I'll give you three reasons why—these eyes, this smile, and this chin. I can sell anything to anybody. Especially sweet, impressionable, single mothers."

Quinn leaned into me. "So the next time you screw up, it's bye-bye, Conrad."

He turned to Sally. "Then it will just be me, your mom, and you, cooking and cleaning. You know how to make nachos, Sally?" Quinn laughed. "You will!"

Behind Quinn, the Cat dropped from the ceiling and started bouncing on the couch again.

"What are you looking at?" Quinn asked. He

spun around, but the Cat was faster. He was back on the ceiling, out of sight. As soon as Quinn turned back around, the Cat dropped to the couch and started bouncing again.

Quinn started to sneeze. "*Achoo!* Is there a cat in here? I'm very allergic to cat hair. *Achoo!*"

"No, no cats in here," I said.

The Cat started scratching behind his ear with his foot, sending up clouds of cat hair.

Quinn was starting to go into convulsions. "*Achoo! Achoo!*"

At the door to the living room, the Fish was leaning out of his kettle, trying to get Quinn's attention. "Hey!" the Fish cried. "He's right above you! Look up! Look—"

The Cat reached down, snagged the kettle with the handle of his umbrella, and yanked the Fish up to the ceiling. Then the Cat grabbed Diver Dan with his tail and dangled him in front of the Fish.

"One more peep out of you," threatened the Cat, "and Diver Dan loses his air supply."

Then the Cat flung the Fish down the hall. "Me-OW!" he crowed.

Quinn froze. "What was that noise? That definitely sounded like a cat!"

Quinn started looking around. Sally and I tried to distract him.

"A cat?" Sally asked.

"Yes, a cat," said Quinn.

"I don't know about that," I said.

"I did not hear a cat," said Sally.

"Certainly not one in a hat," I said.

"A cat in a hat?" Quinn asked.

I started talking fast. "A cat in a hat? I didn't say that. Why in the world would a cat wear a hat?"

Sally talked even faster. "I was standing right here, and I heard what he said. Not a word of a cat with a hat on his head."

Even faster still, I said, "No cat has been here, neither skinny or fat. Right there's where we sat, and we never saw that. We never, ever, ever saw a cat in a hat."

Quinn started sneezing uncontrollably as above him the Cat feverishly scratched his back with both hands, sending down a whirlwind of cat hair.

Sally and I just couldn't help it. We started laughing!

"*Achoo! Achoo!* I'm gonna—*achoo!* And you're gonna—*achoo!* I've got to—*achoo!*—get out of here!"

Quinn ran out the front door. Sally and I were bent over, we were laughing so hard.

"That was amazing!" I finally spluttered.

"We totally got away with it!" said Sally, amazed.

"I told you," said the Cat. "Stick with me, and everything will work out."

At that exact moment the Cat lost his grip on the ceiling and crashed to the floor.

The Cat jumped to his feet, his face scrunched up with pain. "I'm all right, I'm all right. So what do you want to do now?"

"I want to make cupcakes," Sally said.

"Fantastic!" said the Cat. "Cupcakes it is. To the kitchen!"

From all the way down the hall we heard the Fish moan, "Not the kitchen!"

The Cat sat us down in two chairs at the side of the kitchen. Then he disappeared. A voice came out of nowhere and said, "The following is a paid commercial announcement."

We heard a peppy theme song and applause as the Cat ran back into the kitchen. He was wearing a silly-looking multicolored sweater, glasses, and a bad hairpiece.

"Hi," the Cat said. He seemed to be talking to an audience that wasn't there. "Welcome to *Unbelievable Products.* I'm your host, the Guy in the Sweater Who Asks All the Obvious Questions. So, who likes cupcakes?"

"I do," Sally said.

"I do," I chimed in.

"Who doesn't?" the Cat said. "I don't even know why I asked that question. Here now to tell us about his unbelievable product for making cupcakes is the world-famous author of *Cat in the Kitchen and Other Health Code Violations.*"

The Cat held up a cookbook with his face on the cover.

"Please welcome—"

"That's me!" Suddenly the Cat transformed from the show's host to the show's guest, a chef! The Cat's hat was now a red-and-white-striped chef's hat.

Chef Cat said, "Do you love making cupcakes but hate all the hard cupcake work?"

The Cat flipped back into Host mode. "I know *I* do," the Host said.

"Well, forget everything you know about making cupcakes," Chef Cat said, "and say hello to the Amazing Cupcake-inator."

Chef Cat reached under the counter and lifted up a bizarre machine that was part juicer, part Cuisinart, and part cupcake pan.

"Cupcake-a-what?" Host Cat asked.

"Cupcake-inator!" said Chef Cat. "This amazing device will instantly make cupcakes out of anything you have in the kitchen."

"Wait a minute," Host Cat said. "Did you say anything?"

"Anything!" said Chef Cat.

"Anything?" asked Host Cat.

Chef Cat glared at the Host. "Anything!"

There was a moment of silence, then Host Cat said, "Anything?"

Chef Cat looked like his head was going to explode. "I'll get you," he said to the Host menacingly. "Anything! Now come here!"

Chef Cat began stuffing things into the Cupcake-inator. "We'll just throw in a carton of eggs, a pack of hot dogs, a bottle of ketchup, a fire extinguisher, and—hold on—a pinch of hey. . . ."

Chef Cat ran over to Sally and pinched her arm.

"Hey!" Sally said. We watched, amazed, as the word popped out of her mouth like a dialogue bubble in a comic book!

"Thanks!" Chef Cat said. "A Hertz doughnut."

I was wondering what the heck he was talking about when he hit me on the arm.

"Ow!" I cried.

"Hurts, don't it?" Chef Cat asked with a mischievous grin.

Chef Cat ran back to the counter. "Now," he said, "we put all these ingredients in the Cupcake-inator, and delicious cupcakes are just minutes away."

"Did you say minutes away?" Host Cat asked. "That's impossible!"

"You're not just wrong," Chef Cat said, "you're stupid."

Chef Cat turned back to the audience. "Right. We just turn the Cupcake-inator to *bake* and then place it in a conventional oven."

Chef Cat shoved the Cupcake-inator into the oven, power cord and all! Then he slammed the oven shut.

"The beauty of it is," said Chef Cat, "the amazing Cupcake-inator can be yours in just five—"

Chef Cat glanced at his raised hand and the four fingers there.

"—four easy payments," he concluded.

"And if you act now, you'll also get this beautiful set of steak knives."

He held up a set of steak knives.

"These knives won't bend or dull," he said. "And they're so sharp, they can cut through anything."

"Anything?" Host Cat asked.

Chef Cat's face turned red. "Yes! Anything!" He grabbed one of the knives out of the set and chopped it down.

Everybody froze. "Um, Cat?" Sally asked. "Your tail . . ."

Chef Cat looked down. He'd chopped off the end of his tail!

"What about it?" he asked. Suddenly he was just the regular Cat again. "Oh, I see. I've chopped it off. Now, that's interesting, because *aiiiiieee*—"

Everything went black. When the lights came

back up, the Cat was bandaging his tail. Sally and I popped out of our seats as the oven began making an ominous rumbling sound.

"Uh, Cat," I said, "is the oven supposed to be making that sound?"

"Of course," the Cat said. "That means they're almost done, Conrak."

"Conrad," I said, correcting him.

"That's what I said, Condor," said the Cat.

"No, you didn't," I said.

"Of course I did, Convict."

"Cat!" I said.

"Now, that's *my* name," said the Cat.

The Cat pulled out his umbrella and popped it open in front of us just as the oven exploded!

6

Got Cleaning to Do? Try Thing One and Thing Two!

Plates and food for Mom's party flew everywhere.

The Cat lowered his umbrella. Except for the circle protected by the Cat's umbrella, the entire kitchen was coated in dripping purple goop!

"Yep, they're done," the Cat said.

"Oh, man . . . ," I moaned, horrified by the mess. How would we ever clean this up?

"There's nothing to worry about," the Cat said. "I'm sure they still taste fine."

He scooped some purple goop off the wall and put it in his mouth.

"Yuck!" he cried, spitting it out. "Ugh, that's horrible! Who wants some?"

Just then the Fish hopped over in his bowl.

"Aiiieee!" he cried. "I warned you all this would happen."

Sally surveyed the mess. She was suddenly all business. "Cat, you need to clean this up, pronto! We have a contract."

"All right, I'll try," he said.

Sally grabbed the Cat's tie and pulled him down to her level. "You don't try," she said. "You do."

She let go of his tie, and the Cat snapped back upright.

Sometimes it's nice to have the bossiest seven-year-old in town as your sister!

"Yes, ma'am! Right away, ma'am!" the Cat said. "I'll be right back."

The Cat ran out of the room and came back with a large white towel. He started scrubbing at the purple goo.

But there was something odd about the Cat's towel. Sally took a closer look . . . and freaked out!

"Stop!" she cried. "That's not a towel. That's—"

Suddenly I figured it out, too. "Mom's dress!" we screamed together.

The Cat held up the dress. It had a huge purple stain down the front. "This filthy thing?" he asked.

"She was going to wear that tonight!" Sally said. "You ruined it!"

The Fish was moaning in his bowl by the door. "Oh, what will become of us? Your mother will lose her business. And we'll have to live on the street!"

The Cat raised his arms. "Okay, let's everybody take a deep breath and calm down. You know who's going to solve this? *Me. I* am. I will *personally* take care of everything . . . and I know just the guys to do it."

The Cat ran out of the kitchen and down the hall to the front door. We followed him. He returned a moment later dragging a large wooden crate.

"Here we go," the Cat said. He dimmed the lights and a spotlight appeared. The Cat grabbed a spoon and lifted it to his mouth like a microphone. We heard feedback.

"Check, check," the Cat said into the spoon. "Hello, 2434 South Lipplapper Lane! Put your hands together for the answer to all your cleaning needs."

The Cat put his hand on the crate. "In this box are two things. I will show them to you. Two things, and I call them Thing One and Thing Two. These things will not bite you—they want to have fun. So without further ado, meet Thing Two and Thing One!"

The Cat swept off his hat and threw open the crate. Two small, mop-topped creatures jumped out. One wore the number one on his chest; the other wore the number two.

"Dikka dikka depp," said Thing Two.

"Ah, yes. Of course," said the Cat. He turned to Sally and me. "Thing Two would like to clarify that just because he wears the number two, it does not imply in any way that he is inferior to Thing One."

Thing Two continued. "Delippa dikka bapp."

The Cat translated. "He says you may feel free to call him Thing A if you like. He will also accept Super Thing, Thing King, Kid Dynamite, Chocolate Thunda, or Ben."

Thing One spoke up. "Nippa deppa depp."

"Thing One says he's Thing One for a reason, and some people should just get used to it." In a low voice just to Sally and me, the Cat said, "It's a Thing thing. You wouldn't understand."

The Things began jabbering at each other.

"Hey, hey!" the Cat said, getting in between them. "There's no need for that kind of language. There are children in the room."

While the Cat was busy trying to calm down the Things, I sidled over to the Cat's crate. I had to see what was inside! But when I began to lift the lid, something strange started to happen. Everything around the crate started to look distorted and stretched. The wider I opened the lid, the more warped things became. I was about to peer inside the crate when *slam!* the lid came down.

The Cat was glaring at me, his hand on the closed lid of the crate. "Listen, Comdex, you probably don't want to do that."

"Why not?" I asked. "It's just a crate."

"This isn't just any old crate," said the Cat. "This is the Trans-dimensional Transportolator. It's kind of like a doorway that leads from this world to my world."

I pointed at some small type I'd noticed near the top of the crate. "It says 'Made in the Philippines,'" I told him.

"Yes, but not *this* Philippines," the Cat said. "Look, my world and this world really have to stay separate. I'm not a big rules guy, but this is my one: No opening the crate. No lookee, no touchee. Got it?"

The Cat held up a tiny, crablike lock. He placed it near the edge of the crate, and it clamped down, locking the crate shut. Then the Cat

The worst day ever.

Enter the Cat in the Hat!

"Who is this dreadfully uncomfortable woman?"

Conrad and Sally in the cleaning machine.

"We can't spell FUN without *U* in the middle. . . ."

Jumping on the couch—*wahoo!*

Thing 1, Thing 2, and the Cat.

Quinn levels with Conrad and Sally.

The Super Luxurious Omnidirectional Whatchamajigger, or S.L.O.W. for short.

The Mother of All Messes.

Conrad shutting the crate.

The Dynamic Industrial Renovating Tractormajigger—D.I.R.T.!

The cupcakes are a hit.

The best day ever!

slapped a sign on the crate that read, CATS WITH HATS ONLY!

The Cat turned back to the Things. "Now, Things, if you will, follow me, and I'll show you where Sally and Corbin messed up the kitchen."

I lagged behind the group as the Cat led them into the kitchen. Didn't he know better? I wondered. I'm a rule breaker! Now I absolutely *had* to get into that crate!

When they'd gone, I hurried back to the crate and examined the lock. It had a little hole in the middle, sort of like a belly button. I grabbed a paper clip and stuck it in the hole. The crab lock made a weird little grunting noise.

I wiggled the paper clip around a bit, and the crab lock giggled. Finally it popped open. I set it on the floor, where Nevins had come over to investigate. He sniffed at it, and the lock jumped off the floor and attached to Nevins's collar!

Nevins whimpered and ran away, trying to shake the thing off. I made a mental note to help him *after* I'd checked out the crate. I was about to open the lid when the Cat, Sally, and the Things came back into the room with Mom's dress.

I quickly stepped away from the crate and tried to look innocent.

"I don't know why they tried to wipe it up with the dress," the Cat was saying. "Seems foolish to me, too."

Sally was exasperated. "We didn't do it!" she said to the Things. "It was the Cat!"

"They don't speak English," the Cat said to Sally. "Save your breath, tattletale."

He turned back to the Things. "All right, Things, let's get to work! I'm not paying you to stand around and look pretty!"

The Things each took one end of Mom's dress. They jabbered to each other, then snapped the dress hard. The stain flew off the dress . . . and splattered all over the couch!

"There!" the Cat said proudly. "The dress is clean. Nice work, boys. There'll be a little something extra in your paycheck this week."

"What about the couch?" I wanted to know.

"Which couch?" the Cat asked. "The clean one or the horribly stained one?"

The Things produced tennis rackets and began to beat the couch, but the stain didn't budge. Then Thing One grabbed Thing Two and used *him* to beat the couch.

The purple stains flew off the couch and landed on the drapes.

The Fish was watching everything from his bowl. "Dear sweet Mother of Cod! The drapes are destroyed!"

"Trust me," said the Cat, "they did you a favor."

But the Things wouldn't stop. They pulled down the drapes and started swinging them about their heads. Faster and faster the drapes whipped until the purple stains started to fly off . . . splattering the entire room!

"They're wrecking the whole house!" Sally cried.

We had to stop them. They were just making things worse! Then I had an idea. I ran to the closet and opened the door. Mrs. Kwan was still fast asleep, hanging from her hanger. I slid her to one side. Leaning against the back wall of the closet were two large butterfly nets. I grabbed them and handed one to Sally. Then we peeled off in opposite directions. I went after Thing Two, and Sally went after Thing One.

It wasn't pretty. Sally and I chased the Things all over the house, and it just made the mess worse. The Things rode bikes over the furniture and up the walls, leaving purple tread marks everywhere. They ran around the house, flying kites. They even got Mrs. Kwan out of the closet and rode her down the stairs like a toboggan!

I watched as Mrs. Kwan hit the bottom of the stairs and flew through the air, landing right where she'd gone to sleep on the couch! I hefted my net and raced after Thing Two.

Suddenly something grabbed me by the collar. I was dragged to a halt and pulled backward. It was the Cat, and he didn't look happy. He pointed at the crate.

"Klondike? Do you have any idea what happened to the lock on this crate?" he asked.

"No," I said. "And I'm a little busy."

The Cat narrowed his eyes at me.

"Okay!" I said. "I was curious, so I picked the lock. I was going to lock it again, I swear."

"We really need that back," the Cat said. "Where is it?"

"It's on Nevins's collar," I said sheepishly.

"Nevins?" the Cat asked.

Suddenly from behind us Sally cried out, "Nevins! They've got Nevins!"

The Cat and I turned to see Thing Two holding Nevins. He and Thing One were examining him curiously. I noticed the crab lock was still clamped to Nevins's collar.

"Put him down!" Sally ordered. "Are you deaf? I said put the dog down! Why won't they listen to me?"

The Cat settled back onto the couch next to

the sleeping Mrs. Kwan. He sipped at a fruity drink with a slice of pineapple and a little umbrella stuck in it.

"Oh, I don't know if this will help," the Cat said, "but the Things always do the opposite of what you say."

The Cat glanced at me and gestured at his drink. "Should I use a coaster?"

I was studying the Things and frowning. "Why do they always do the opposite?" I asked. "That's so annoying."

Sally gave me a look. "Remind you of anyone, Conrad?"

"Zinger!" said the Cat.

I scowled. I should have seen that one coming.

Thing One lined up behind Thing Two, and they both crouched like football players.

"Blue meppa-two!" Thing One called out. "Dakka-fourteen! Hut hut hike!"

Thing Two snapped Nevins back to Thing One as if he were a football and went out for the pass.

"Hey, Things!" Sally said. "*Don't* let go of that dog!"

I glanced at my sister in admiration. Good thinking!

The Things paused and looked at each other. Thing One said, "Nekka bekka *don't* let go."

Then their faces lit up. Together they cried, "Let go!"

Thing Two reared back and hurled Nevins across the room!

"Catch him!" I cried. "I mean, *don't* catch him! *Don't* catch him! Aiigh!"

It was too late. Thing One watched with folded arms as Nevins flew right out the window!

Sally and I ran to the window. Horrified, we watched as Nevins scampered across the street and disappeared.

7
Cat Chases Dog

Sally was beside herself. "Well, this is just great, Conrad. The whole house is destroyed, the party's ruined, and now Nevins is gone."

"Oh, sure," I said. "There's a six-foot cat and two blue-haired midgets in long johns having a decathlon in the house, and it's my fault."

The Cat walked over. "Sally, Kojak, that's nothing compared to what's going to happen if we don't lock this crate. Take a look—it's already leaking!"

He was right. Purple goop was dripping down one side of the crate. As we watched, it reached the carpet. Instantly the design on the carpet came to life, growing weird, vibrantly colored tentacles!

Sally and I ran over and pushed the lid closed, but the goop just forced it open again.

"It won't stay shut," I said.

"Not without the lock," said the Cat. "If we don't get that lock off Nevins and put it back on this crate, we're going to be staring down the business end of the Mother of All Messes."

Sally and I looked at each other, stunned. I can't be sure what she was thinking, but I know I couldn't believe our fun could have such horrible consequences.

There was only one thing to do. "We've got to go out there and find Nevins," I said.

"Come on!" the Cat said. "Let's go get that dog. Now, we just need a heavy inanimate object to weigh down this crate. . . ."

A few minutes later, we were ready to go. We'd decided to use Mrs. Kwan to keep the lid shut! She was snoring away on top of the crate.

"That ought to buy us some time," the Cat said. "Now, let's go go go!"

Sally and I ran out the door. We hadn't gone ten steps before I realized the Cat wasn't with us.

"Wait a minute," I said, and ran back to the door. Inside, the Cat was speaking into a hand-held tape recorder.

"Kitchen a mess, check," he said. "Kids outside, check. Right on schedule."

Huh? I thought. *What's that all about?*

I shook my head and followed Sally. The Cat came through the door behind me. He looked left, then right, then did a ninja roll and sprang to his feet.

"Are you sure you should be coming with us?" Sally asked.

"Of course," the Cat said. "I'm an indoor/outdoor cat."

"What if someone notices we're gone?" Sally said.

"Don't worry," said the Cat. "I've got that covered. I'm so smart."

As we headed across the street, I looked back at the front of the house. It looked like Sally and

I were sitting in the big bay window, reading!

How? I wondered. Then I knew. It was Thing One and Thing Two!

We followed the Cat around to the backyards across the street and peered over our neighbor's fence. Nevins was sniffing around the bushes!

"Okay, there's Nevins," I said. "Everyone stay out of sight."

The Fish was in a jelly jar full of water at the top of my backpack. He scowled. "For the record, I strongly object to this foray. And I resent being dragged along as an accomplice."

The Cat started stretching. He cracked every joint in his body, even his hat!

"Get outta my way," he said. "This fence is no match for my catlike grace and reflexes. Watch me fly!"

A few minutes later, the Cat was still trying to get over the fence—using me and Sally to push off of!

"Ow!" I said as the Cat planted his knee in my face.

"Just a little higher," the Cat said. He put his foot on Sally's head. "I don't think the little girl is even trying."

"What about your catlike reflexes?" Sally asked.

"What about you showing a little effort, shrimp boat? Push!"

Sally and I heaved, and the Cat went flying over the fence. We watched as he bounced up and grabbed a hoe off the lawn.

"All right, Nevins," he said. "Time to die!"

Sally and I looked at each other. *What?!?*

The Cat charged at Nevins. Sally and I jumped the fence as Nevins gave a yelp of terror and ran in the opposite direction.

"Cat, you scared him away!" I yelled as we chased after him.

"Oh, right. Sorry," said the Cat. He started calling, "Good doggie. Nice doggie. Come back. Please. I'm begging you."

We chased Nevins through backyard after backyard. Finally we caught up with him. He was in someone's backyard, jumping for a pack of uncooked hot dogs sitting next to a barbecue. A piñata was hanging from a tree in the middle of the yard.

"There he is," I said.

Sally glanced at the house. "Hey . . ."

Inside the house a party was going on. A HAPPY BIRTHDAY banner was hanging from the ceiling, and colorful balloons were taped to the walls. The room was full of kids Sally's age, playing and eating cake. In the middle of it all was a familiar-looking girl. . . .

"Denise?" Sally said. My sister looked shocked. "Everyone I know is there. Ginny and Ellen and . . . even the dumb Schweitzer kid?"

We watched as Schweitzer walked toward the lit birthday candles like a robot. "I am a robot. Beep. I am impervious to flame. Beep."

Sally looked hurt. "How come Denise didn't invite *me* to her birthday?"

"Maybe because you told her to never speak to you again," I suggested.

From inside the house I heard the Schweitzer kid say, "Ow. Sensors indicate heat."

Sally looked crushed.

"Look, don't worry about it," I said. "Let's just get Nevins and go."

Suddenly we heard Denise's mom say, "Okay, kids! Everyone outside!"

Sally and I looked at each other in terror.

"Hide!" I said.

Nevins darted away as Sally and I dove behind two small bushes. There was nowhere for the Cat to hide!

"Cat, they're going to see you!" I said.

The Cat looked around in a panic. I looked over at the house—the kids were coming out! When I looked back, the Cat was hanging by a string from the tree, imitating the piñata.

"Piñata!" the kids cried. They circled the Cat, and Sally's friend Denise was pushed forward. She was blindfolded and holding a whiffle bat.

Denise took a few swings at the Cat. The Cat managed to twist himself out of the way each time until finally Denise smacked him on the head—*whack!*

"Hit it harder!" the kids cried.

"Everybody join me!" Denise said.

The kids cheered. They grabbed whiffle bats and started whaling away on the Cat!

"It's breaking . . . ," Denise said as stuff started to fall out of the Cat's pockets.

Sally and I watched, helpless, from behind our bushes.

Then we heard the Schweitzer kid say, "Step out of the way."

The crowd of kids parted to let through the Schweitzer kid. He was holding a jumbo-sized whiffle bat. He took careful aim.

The Cat waved a tiny white flag in surrender.

The Schweitzer kid wound up and . . . *WHACK!*

"Hey!" the Cat cried.

The kids all froze. Sally and I looked at each other. Oh, no! They'd seen the Cat! What were we going to do?

Glancing around, I saw the real piñata beside me and got an idea. Only one thing in the world could make these kids forget what they'd seen. I broke open the piñata and pulled out a handful of—

"Candy!" I yelled.

The kids all looked up. "Candy?!?" they cried.

I started tossing handfuls of candy into the air. The kids forgot about the Cat in a mad scramble to get as much candy as they could.

While the kids were distracted, Sally, the Cat, and I slipped out to the street and hid behind a hedge. The Cat's hat transformed to a periscope. The Cat poked it over the hedge and peered through.

"All right, soldiers," the Cat said in a southern accent. "Our bogey is in range. Commence search and destroy."

"What?" I asked.

"Search and *rescue,*" said the Cat. "I meant search and *rescue.*"

"I can't believe I wasn't invited to that party," Sally said.

"Hey, they did you a favor," said the Cat. "You would have hated it. All those people who don't do exactly what you say eating cake, laughing their heads off, and having a great time? You don't need that."

"I guess not . . . ," Sally said doubtfully.

"Hey. You're a lone wolf," the Cat said. "Makes me wish I wasn't so popular. Always surrounded by friends, bathed in love, building cherished memories. It's a pain."

"Can we please get the dog?" I said.

We all peered over the hedge. Nevins was across the street, sniffing at a fire hydrant. Suddenly a car pulled up next to Nevins. It was a Thunderbird!

"Oh, no . . . ," I said.

Sure enough, Quinn got out. "Well, well, well," he said.

Quinn grabbed Nevins and held him up to his

face. “Not so tough now, are you?” he asked the dog. “Boy, is Joan going to be steamed when she finds out Conrad lost the family dog again. *Bon voyage,* Private Conrad!”

We watched as Quinn stuffed Nevins in the car and drove off.

8

The Cat in the Hat Has a Car That's All That

"We're dead," I moaned. "We're never going to get that crate shut, and I'm getting shipped off to Colonel von Kronk's School for Wayward Boys."

Sally started to cry. "Where's he going with Nevins? What's he going to do to him?"

From his jelly jar in my backpack, the Fish was watching everything. "Be strong, Sally," he said. Then *he* started to cry. "Oh, what's the use? All is lost! Whatever are we to do?"

"Why don't we take my car?" the Cat asked.

"You have a car?" I said.

The Cat pulled out a garage door opener and pressed the button. Next to us appeared a freestanding one-car garage. The door opened, revealing a super-cool, space-age bullet car! It was gleaming with high-tech gadgetry.

"Wow!" I said. "That is so cool!"

"That's just the dust cover," the Cat boasted. "Here she is!"

The Cat walked over and yanked away the bullet-car tarp.

Underneath was a rickety, three-wheeled vehicle that looked like a junkyard had coughed it up.

"The Super Luxurious Omnidirectional Whatchamajigger," the Cat said proudly. "Or S.L.O.W. for short. Quick! To the S.L.O.W.!"

We hopped in. On the dashboard was a Cat bobble head doll. A giant seat belt swung across both me and Sally and strapped us in.

"Buckle up, kids," said the Cat. "We're on a mission to get that dog, and we will not rest until we find it and destroy it!"

"Rescue it," I corrected.

"Rescue it," said the Cat. "Right."

The Cat grabbed the Fish's jelly jar and

slapped it on the roof like a police light. Then he stepped on the gas. As we drove away, the Fish's screams sounded like a siren!

S.L.O.W. chugged along. The Cat was wearing old-fashioned aviator goggles and a red-and-white-striped scarf. His hat stuck out of the sunroof.

"There they are!" the Cat said, pointing straight ahead. "No one can outrun S.L.O.W.!"

Sure enough, Quinn's car was going through the intersection ahead of us.

The Cat stepped on the gas. Sally and I cheered.

We were headed toward the intersection, fast. Sally and I screamed as S.L.O.W. started to spin and swerve to avoid other cars.

But somehow we got through the intersection unharmed.

From the roof the Fish called, "You're going to get us all killed! Do you even have a driver's license?"

The Cat showed us his license. In the photo

the Cat had an Afro and a mustache. It read, LAST NAME: IN THE HAT. FIRST NAME: CAT.

The Fish quickly scanned the license. "This license has expired!" he said. "And you're not wearing your corrective lenses! I refuse to let you drive."

"All right, you win," said the Cat. He turned to me. "Concrete, you drive."

The Cat slid the steering wheel across the dash to my side of the car.

Cool!

I grabbed the wheel and tried to steer, but the car bucked all over the road, and the gears were grinding.

"How am I supposed to do this?" I asked.

"Where's your imagination?" the Cat asked. "Haven't you ever pretended you're a race car driver? Make the noise. Vrrrrr!"

I shrugged. Feeling a little silly, I gave it a try. "Vrrrrr . . ."

Immediately the car jumped forward. The stick shift moved by itself into a higher gear.

"See?" the Cat said. "There you go. Now punch it!"

Yes! I thought. I made higher and higher revving sounds. The car did an amazing 360 spin, then shot down the street.

"This is awesome!" I crowed.

Up ahead I could see Quinn's car. We were gaining on him! Then Sally poked me.

"I want to drive," she said.

"Oh, sorry," I sneered, "but I checked your PalmPilot. It's not on your schedule."

"I want to drive!" Sally screamed.

"That's a great idea!" said the Cat.

The Cat pressed a button on the dash, and a steering wheel popped up in front of Sally.

"Yeah!" Sally said. "Vrrrrr!"

The car started to swerve as both Sally and I tried to control it.

"Two people can't drive at the same time!" I screamed.

"You're right," said the Cat. "It's not enough people. We should *all* drive."

The Cat pulled out another steering wheel and stuck it onto the dash in front of him. Even the *Fish* had a little steering wheel. He made little bubbling engine noises.

The car veered crazily from side to side.

"Cat!" I yelled desperately. "Where are the brakes?"

"I'll get them," the Cat said. He reached under the dash, ripped out the brake pedal, and held it up.

S.L.O.W. spun out of control into the town square.

Honk, honk!

"Truck!" Sally and I both screamed.

"Hey, a Rhode Island license plate," said the Cat. "You never see those."

We all turned our wheels hard—in different directions! S.L.O.W. bounced off the curb and started to spin again.

"Aaaaiiiggghhh!" we all screamed.

We spun right past where Quinn was parking his car and crashed into a light post. *Crunch!*

There was a moment of silence, then the Cat's hat inflated like an air bag.

Sally and I climbed out of the wrecked car. "Can we do that again?" I asked.

The Fish's jelly jar rolled out of the wreckage. He looked pale. "I think I wet my jar," he said.

The Cat sprang up. "Great parking space!" he said. "Now let's go find that unpleasant pet of yours."

We peered around the corner and saw Quinn lift Nevins out of his car, then walk into a store called Safari Sam's Big Screen Jungle. A sign in the window read, IF YOU WANT TO BAG BIG GAME OR WATCH THE BIG GAME, COME ON IN!

We hurried down the sidewalk and peered through the window. It was an electronics store with jungle decorations. There were fake animal skins on the floor and elephant tusks and woven grass mats on the walls.

We watched as Quinn walked over to a salesperson dressed in khaki-colored hunting clothes and a pith helmet that was a few sizes too big.

"Welcome to the jungle—we've got what you need!" said the salesperson. "I am Sanjay, and I will be your guide on a bargain safari. Can I help you bag the big one today?"

"Don't do that," Quinn said.

"Very good, sir," said Sanjay.

Quinn pointed to a TV. "I want to talk to you about this TV," he said.

"Oh, no, sir," said Sanjay. "You do not want that one. Perhaps I can put you into a big screen?"

"Well, I can't really afford to—" Quinn paused, then said, "What if I told you I wanted to put a little down now, somewhere in the two-to-four-dollar range, and come back and pay off the whole thing in a few weeks?"

"You are planning on winning the lottery?" Sanjay asked.

"Better," Quinn said. "I'm going to ask my girlfriend to marry me."

I felt my stomach drop. Sally's face turned white. The Fish popped out of his jar.

"I told you!" he said self-righteously. "This

is what happens when you jump on the couch."

Inside, Quinn held up Nevins and said, "Thanks to this dog here, her brat kid's going off to military school, and I'm gonna turn his bedroom into a home theater. Show me the biggest system you got."

Quinn tied up Nevins with a video cable, then followed Sanjay into the back of the store. The coast was clear. Sally, the Fish, the Cat, and I slipped into the store.

I quickly untied Nevins. "Welcome back, Nevins!" I said. "We missed you!"

Nevins licked our faces as Sally and I hugged him.

"Uch, that's disgusting," said the Cat. "He's an animal. Who knows where he's been?"

"All right, let's get out of—" I started to say. Then we heard Quinn and Sanjay coming back! Sally and I hid in cabinets on either side of a big-screen TV. The Cat looked around frantically. Once again, he had nowhere to hide. Finally he just dropped to the floor.

"Excellent choice, Mr. Quinn," Sanjay was saying. "Let's just write up the order."

As Quinn and Sanjay walked across the room, I saw that the Cat was disguising himself as an animal rug! His body was flat, but his head remained full-size.

Quinn and Sanjay walked onto the Cat. The Cat was about to yell, but I peeked out of my cabinet and caught his eye.

"Please, Mr. Quinn," Sanjay said. "Sit down."

Sanjay grabbed two desk chairs and rolled them onto the Cat. The two men sat down.

"Let me grab a pen," said Sanjay. He rolled his chair across the Cat to a desk, picked up a pen, then rolled back.

Suddenly Quinn sneezed. "*Achoo!* Is there a cat around here?"

"Oh, no," said Sanjay. "Very bad luck. And the smell. Very unclean creatures."

The Cat scowled and started to reach for Sanjay, but a look from Sally stopped him.

"So when will this baby come in?" Quinn was asking.

"Let me find out," Sanjay said. "Maria!"

A woman in high-heeled shoes walked out from the back. She was smoking a cigarette.

"I'm on my break," the woman said, stepping onto the Cat.

"Maria, I told you, no smoking in here!" said Sanjay. "The grass mats will go up in an instant! Put that out!"

Maria rolled her eyes, dropped her cigarette onto the Cat, and stamped it out with her shoe.

The Cat looked furious!

"Make sure it's out!" Sanjay said.

Maria stomped down harder.

Sanjay turned back to Quinn. "Let me ask someone in the shipping department about your television. Hey, Tiny!"

We heard a *bam-bam-bam,* and a giant guy came bouncing into the room on a pogo stick.

"Tiny, what are you doing?" Sanjay asked.

"I'm trying to set the record!" Tiny said. He was on his way toward the Cat when the Cat finally decided he'd had enough.

"No way!" the Cat said. "That's it!"

Everyone toppled to the ground as the Cat pulled himself out from under them. I jumped out of my cabinet and grabbed Nevins, and we all headed for the door.

Behind us Quinn yelled, "Come back here, you little maggots!"

As we flew out the door, the Cat pulled a smoking cigarette butt out of his fur and flicked it away. Then we headed down the street at full speed. Quinn charged out after us.

"Come back here!" he yelled.

The chase was on!

9

One Hat, Two Hat, Three Hat, Four Hat!

We ran down the street with Quinn hard on our tail.

Around the corner was a door. We darted inside and found ourselves in a huge dance club! The music was thumping, and the air was full of smoke and laser light. The floor was packed full of dancers, all wearing glow stick necklaces and funky clothing. Best of all, almost everyone was wearing a hat just like the Cat's!

We quickly dove into the crowd as Quinn followed us through the door. As we made our way through the dancers, we watched Quinn tackle a tall guy in a Cat hat. I grinned. It'd worked! But we all must have been watching Quinn and not looking where we were going, because the next thing I knew, we'd run straight into a bunch of clubgoers. We all fell down amid a pile of Cat hats.

The Cat jumped back up and started looking over the hats, trying to find his. I glanced back. Quinn had spotted us!

"C'mon, Cat!" I said. The Cat grabbed a hat out of the pile as Sally and I dragged him out of the club.

We sprinted out the back door. Finally we stopped to catch our breath behind a statue. We looked around. There was no sign of Quinn.

"I think we lost him," Sally said.

I took the lock off Nevins's collar.

"We got the lock back," I said. "Let's get home."

Suddenly I froze.

"What's wrong?" Sally asked.

I pointed across the street. It was Mom's office. Mom was walking out—with Quinn!

"Joan, your children are running around town like maniacs with some weird, hairy guy in a hat!" he said. "You'll believe everything I've been saying to you as soon as we get to your house. Come on."

As we watched, Quinn and Mom got into her car and drove off.

"Cat, we've got to get home before they do," I said. "Do something!"

"I'm on it," the Cat said. He took off his hat and knocked on it three times. Then he reached into it. A puzzled look came over his face.

"Hey . . . ," he said.

"What's wrong?" I asked.

The Cat looked up at me in total surprise. "This . . . this is not my hat. . . ."

10
Race Her, Chase Her—Get Moving and Outpace Her!

The Cat shook his head, bewildered. "I must have picked up the wrong hat back there."

I grabbed the hat and looked inside. "But it says 'Made in the Philippines,'" I said.

"Yes," said the Cat. "But unfortunately, that's *your* Philippines."

"So?" Sally asked.

"So without the hat," said the Cat, "I'm just your garden-variety six-foot-tall talking cat."

"You're totally powerless?" I asked.

The Cat shrugged. "Not totally," he said. "I can still tell you the capitals of all forty-two states."

"There's fifty," Sally said.

The Cat looked stunned. "We're doomed!" he said.

I felt my shoulders slump in defeat. "We're dead," I said. "This is all my fault. I'm such an idiot. Why do I always do the opposite of what I'm supposed to?"

I suddenly had a brilliant idea! "Wait a second," I said. "That's it. The opposite!

"Things!" I yelled at the top of my voice. "*Don't* help us! *Do not* show up and help us get home right now!"

Sally was opening her mouth—about to say something smart, I'm sure—when a car horn honked from down the street. A moment later, Quinn's Thunderbird pulled up! The doors opened, and out hopped the Things! They were wearing little red vests, like the valets who park cars at restaurants and hotels.

"Midda peppa meppadap?" asked Thing One, stepping aside and holding open the door.

"We've got a chance to beat them back to the

house now," I said. "Everybody get in!"

The car was a little small for all of us, but we scrambled in anyway. I jumped into the driver's seat.

I drove fast. Considering that I'd never driven a real car before, it was pretty scary. I glanced in the rearview mirror. The Things had their heads out of the back windows, their faces pointing into the wind like dogs. The Cat was wedged in between them, holding the imposter hat in his lap and moping.

"How we doing on time?" I asked as we screeched around a corner.

"Time?" the Cat asked. "Time's up. Game over, man! All aboard the give-up train! That crate's been open all day and that house is going to be the Mother of All Messes, man! And your mom's going to be home any second! Look at the PalmPilot. We don't have enough time!"

Sally clenched her fist. "Forget the stupid PalmPilot! I've been a slave to that thing for—"

She checked the PalmPilot.

"—412.3 days! Step on it, Conrad. We can do this!"

Then Sally tossed her PalmPilot out the window! I stared at her, amazed. She looked me right in the eye and smiled. I smiled back. We were going to do it!

Then Sally stared out the window. "There's Mom and Quinn!" she said.

I glanced over. Sure enough, Mom and Quinn were on a parallel street a block away.

I looked into the rearview mirror. "Hey, Things. *Do not* do anything to slow down my mom."

The Things looked at each other and grinned excitedly. Then they jumped out of the car and ran off.

"The Hat would have loved that plan," said the Cat sadly.

I took a quick right, then another left. Now we were behind Mom and Quinn. As we watched, the Things pulled up behind them on a police motorcycle with the siren on! Mom pulled over.

Way to go, Things! I thought as we sped by. I was starting to think we had a chance.

Soon we were pulling up in front of our house. Sally and I grabbed the Fish and Nevins, and we all hopped out. We were running up the front steps . . . when Quinn jumped out of the bushes!

11

This Is the House the Cat Built

How did he beat us here? I wondered.

"Not so fast, you maggots!" Quinn snarled. Before we could react, he'd grabbed me and Sally. I quickly glanced around. The Cat had disappeared!

"You are stone-cold busted," Quinn said. "Get inside."

Quinn shoved us toward the front door.

"Trust me," I said. "You really don't want to go in there. It's gonna be a total—"

My voice caught as Quinn pushed me through the door.

"—wreck?" I finished lamely.

The house was spotless! I looked at my sister in bewilderment.

"Your mom's gonna be home any minute," Quinn said. "By the time I get through telling her all the stunts you pulled today, there are going to be *two* new cadets in the family."

Sally started to cry. I hung my head in defeat.

Quinn started to gloat. "Sally, maybe I'll turn your old room into a gym. Or maybe a second TV room—*achoo! Achoo!* Why am I sneezing?"

My heart jumped with hope as I heard the Cat say from behind us, "That'd be me."

Quinn spun around. A look of disbelief and terror crossed his face. "You're a giant—*achoo!*—cat!"

"Again, I really prefer 'big-boned,'" the Cat said.

Quinn staggered back in fear. As he hit the wall, it ripped like paper! Quinn fell through the hole and disappeared. We heard his scream coming from farther and farther away. Then all the walls fell away, and we saw what was happening.

The floor of the entryway was suspended high up in the air, as if we were standing on a mountain peak! Thousands of feet below us floated oddly shaped clouds. Quinn got smaller and smaller until he disappeared into them.

"So *this* is the Mother of All Messes," I said.

"Yep," said the Cat. "Pure, unadulterated fun without my good sense and judgment. We're looking at a too-much-fun house!"

The Fish spluttered. "I told you this would happen!" he said. "It's *exactly* as I predicted."

Sally and I gave the Fish a skeptical look.

"Well, perhaps not *exactly,*" said the Fish. "My version didn't have as many mountains. . . ."

I just shook my head. "Come on," I said. The hall carpet was stretched out over all that empty space like a bridge. We started across. Before long we came to a window suspended in midair. I parted the curtains and looked out.

It couldn't have looked more normal outside. Somebody rode by on a bike, saw me, and waved. I waved back. Weird!

We continued on, and it wasn't long before we came to the family room—or what had been the family room. Now it was more like a fun house, with multiple levels and zigzagging stairs and ladders going every which way. Nothing was the size it should be—the table at the end of the couch had become teeny tiny, while the lamp that sat on it had become gigantic! Through the middle of it all ran a river of purple carpet over a set of jagged stairs.

"On the plus side," said the Cat, "I think people will talk about tonight's party for the rest of their lives."

"We've got to shut that crate," Sally said. "How do we find it?"

"We follow the mess back to the source," I said.

We looked around, trying to tell from which direction the mess had come. That's when we saw Mrs. Kwan, floating along in the purple river. She was still asleep. In fact, she was snoring!

The Cat grabbed her and held her steady next to the bank of the river. "Hop on," he said.

"We're going to ride Mrs. Kwan?" I asked.

"If you're tall enough," the Cat said. Suddenly there was a sign beside us that said, YOU MUST BE THIS TALL TO RIDE THE KWAN. Sally was shorter than the mark on the sign, but the Cat held her up so that she was tall enough. Then we all stepped onto Mrs. Kwan!

"Keep your hands and feet in the Kwan at all times," the Cat said. Mrs. Kwan started to float toward the stairs. As we rode the purple river up the stairs, we heard the *clickity-clack* sound a roller coaster makes on its way up a hill.

At the top of the stairs were rapids. As we thundered through them, we stared in amazement at the warped landscape that had been our house.

"Is that the hallway bathroom?" Sally asked.

I looked over and saw a grumbling toilet suddenly erupt like a volcano! It blew flames a hundred feet into the sky!

Suddenly the purple river dropped, and we were hurtling down the rapids on a Mrs. Kwan flume ride!

"Ahhhhhh!" Sally and I screamed.

The Cat lifted his arms over his head. "You get a much wilder ride in the *back* of the Kwan."

We splashed into a purple pool at the bottom of the hill and drifted into what had been the living room. The furniture was huge and towered overhead. The ceiling was lost somewhere high above us. The walls breathed in and out!

Mrs. Kwan came to a stop.

"I think this is it," I said.

"There's the crate!" Sally said.

Sure enough, at the far end of the room was the crate. The purple river was pouring out of it.

"Let's get this crate shut, and the house will be back to normal," I said.

Sally and I grabbed the lid and tried to force it down, but the purple river was pushing against us! Then the Cat joined us.

"It's closing!" the Cat cried.

A vortex of light and wind sprang up and began sucking all the weirdness back into the crate. The mountains shrank and the wild stairways retracted. There was a final burst of blinding light, and *pow,* the lid was closed.

I slammed the lock back on the crate, and its pincers snapped into place. The crate shuddered once or twice, as if something was trying to get out. But the lock held.

I looked at Sally, and she grinned at me. We'd done it!

"That was easy," I said.

"I did it!" the Cat crowed. "I did it!"

The Cat noticed that Sally and I were giving him a look.

"Okay, we did it," he said lamely.

Sally looked around. "I don't think we did anything. . . ."

I turned. All the Cat's magic had been sucked back into the crate, so the house was back to normal . . . its normal *mess.* The place was totaled!

12

It's Fun to Have Fun, but Enough Is Enough!

I looked around the room in disbelief. It looked like a tornado had hit! Bookshelves were overturned, furniture was destroyed . . . even a staircase was missing!

This wasn't the way it was supposed to work! I turned to the Cat. "The place is still a wreck," I said. "Cat, you said if we shut the crate, everything would be okay. But it's not. It's a complete disaster!"

"Hmmm," said the Cat. He walked over to a picture on the wall that was slightly askew and delicately straightened it. "How about now?"

As he turned to look at us, the wall the picture

was hung on broke apart and collapsed.

"What game should we play next?" the Cat asked. "Tennis, anyone?"

The Cat pulled some tennis rackets out of his hat. Suddenly he was wearing sweatbands and a headband.

"This scorch mark is the sideline," said the Cat, "and that collapsed wall can be the net."

"Hey!" I said, giving the Cat a suspicious look. "Your hat! It's magic again!"

The Cat pretended to look shocked. "Oops! You caught me!" he said. He winked. "You can serve first."

I was shocked. "You had your real hat this whole time?"

"So you just pretended you couldn't help us?" Sally asked.

"Yep!" the Cat said, beaming at us. "And wasn't that a lot more fun? You guys did great! I'll be honest, I was afraid you were going to catch the Things before they could throw Nevins out the window."

"Wait a second," Sally said. "You knew they would do that?"

"Of course I did!" the Cat said. "I planned the whole day!"

"The house getting trashed," Sally said, "Quinn taking Nevins, all of it?"

"Yep," said the Cat. "I even got your mother out of the house."

Sally shook her head. "No, she had an appointment with Mr. Filene."

"It's pronounced 'Fee-line,'" the Cat said.

"*That* was you?" I asked.

"It was *all* me," the Cat said. "I planned everything! Except chopping off the end of my tail. That was not in the playbook."

The Cat looked glumly at his bandaged tail.

I was trying to take it all in. "You even knew I'd open the crate?" I asked.

"Why do you think I made it my one rule?" the Cat asked. "I knew you couldn't resist."

Suddenly I remembered when I had caught the

Cat talking into his tape recorder. Now things were starting to make sense!

"Well," the Cat said, "now that the cat's out of the bag, to use an archaic and cruel-sounding metaphor, how about that game of tennis?"

"'Game'?" I said. I was starting to get angry. "The house is destroyed. You said nothing bad would happen."

"Yeah, we had a contract," said Sally.

The Cat cleared his throat. "Oh, right," he said. "About that contract . . ."

The Cat whipped out the contract. Out of his hat shot a mechanical arm holding a magnifying glass. The Cat studied the contract through it.

"Section 7, paragraph B, subsection 894 of the addendum to the addendum of the second part of the first agreement, down there near the jelly stain," said the Cat. From the contract he read: "The contract will be null and void if Conrad—a.k.a. Gorman—chooses to open the crate and loses the lock."

The Cat looked up at us. "Sorry. Should have had your lawyers look it over. Now, who's up for Canadian doubles?"

I'd had enough. Quietly but firmly, I said, "Get out."

The Cat looked puzzled. "I don't know that game," he said.

"It's not a game," I said. "None of this is a game."

"What are we supposed to tell our mother?" Sally asked. "Cat, you need to go."

The Cat looked surprised. "But I thought you two wanted to have fun today."

"Look around, Cat!" I said. "You were right—it's fun to have fun, but you have to know how. And you don't know when enough is enough. Now go!"

"Suzy, Cromwell, please—" the Cat began.

"Out!" Sally and I shouted.

The Cat could tell we meant business. He sighed. Lowering his head, he grabbed the crate and pulled it through the front door. Just like that, he was gone, and Sally and I were on our own.

That's right, I said *Sally and I.* Somehow, something had changed. After the events of the day, I felt differently toward my sister. I think she felt different about me, too.

"Good riddance!" said the Fish. "Now, this may not be the time for 'I told you so,' but—"

Sally and I glared at the Fish.

"Like I said," said the Fish. "Not the time."

Sally and I looked over the mess. "I'll get the mop and bucket," Sally said. "Conrad, you might want to get out of here until Mom has a chance to calm down."

For just a moment, I considered following my sister's advice. But for only a moment.

"No," I said. "This was all my fault. I'll take the blame. Look, Mom will be home any second. Why don't you go upstairs?"

"I'm not going upstairs," Sally said firmly. "I'm staying with you."

"Really?" I said. "Why?"

"Two reasons," Sally said. "One, the stairs have been destroyed."

Good reason, I thought.

"And two," Sally continued, "this is just as much my fault as yours. We should share the blame."

Then Sally took my hand and smiled at me. Yes, it was definitely the start of a new era between us. Makes you a little sick, doesn't it?

"Thanks, Sal," I said. Had I ever called her "Sal" before? Ugh! But what can you do? When your sister's cool, she's cool.

Then we heard the sound of a car pulling up outside. Headlights flashed into the room. I took a deep breath.

"By the way," Sally said. "You're a pretty good brother."

"I'm glad you think that," I said. "Maybe we can room together at military school."

We heard the key turn in the lock and watched the doorknob start to turn.

"Well, here goes . . . ," I said.

13
The Cat in the Hat Comes Back!

It was the Cat! He rode through the door on a . . . well, I'm not sure what you'd call it. It looked a lot like S.L.O.W., except this machine was part riding mower and part street cleaner and had all sorts of mechanical arms holding brooms and dustpans and rags.

"Cat?" Sally asked.

The Cat whipped out the contract again. "Section 8, article 93, subparagraph 834. By the other jelly stain," he said.

The magnifying glass popped out of his hat and positioned itself over the contract. Through it, the Cat read: "If Sally and Conrad learn from their mistakes, the contract shall be reinstated."

The Cat looked up at us. "And I think you two have satisfied the legal burden of learning. Now let's play one last game. It's called Clean Up the House."

The Cat gestured at the machine he was riding. "Kids, meet the Dynamic Industrial Renovating Tractormajigger."

Sally and I looked at each other. "D.I.R.T.?" we both asked.

"That's right!" the Cat said. "Out of the way. Nothing cleans better than D.I.R.T.!"

Then through the door came Thing One and Thing Two on their own mini–cleaning machines! The Things were dressed in racing janitor outfits.

Sally and I cheered. The Fish cried, "I knew he'd come back! I knew he'd help us!"

Everyone stopped and looked at the Fish.

"What?" the Fish said. "I did!"

The Cat and the Things sprang into cleaning action. As they worked, the Cat sang a cleaning song.

"I always pick up
My playthings and so . . .
I will show you another
Good trick that I know . . .
Because D.I.R.T. cleans up
Even faster than S.L.O.W.!"

As we watched, D.I.R.T. mopped and dusted and repainted! It sucked up Mom's dress. When it spit it out, the dress was dry-cleaned and perfect. It even grabbed us, gave us a scrubbing, and put new clothes on us!

The Cat sang:

"Together we can pick up
All the things that are down.
We can pick up the plates
And the books and the gown
And the milk and the strings."

"And the eggs!" Sally sang.

"And the dish!" I joined in.

Thing One and Thing Two were cleaning the

fishbowl and cried, "Neppa fan! Dekka cup! Deppa ship! Neppa Fish!"

"Don't forget Diver Dan!" called the Fish.

We heard a car, and Sally ran over to the window. "Mom just pulled into the driveway!" she cried.

The Things zipped into the kitchen. Their machines swept up the shards of glass and the mounds of food glop and left behind stacks of clean plates and perfect trays of hors d'oeuvres.

The Cat sang:

> "We'll re-pit the olives
> And re-bake the cake.
> I'll tack up these drapes,
> But they're still a mistake."

The Cat hung up the drapes and made a face.

> "We'll re-plaster the ceiling,
> Repair the commode.
> We'll re-plumb the plumbing.
> It'll all be to code."

S.L.O.W. picked up Mrs. Kwan and spun her so fast that all the muck flew off of her. Then the machine blow-dried and brushed her hair. Finally it put her down gently on the now spotless white couch.

Sally was still at the window, watching Mom. "She's getting the mail!" Sally shouted. "Now she's coming up the walk!"

The Cat was unfazed.

"We'll un-dirty the dirt."

"It's working, thank heavens!" said the Fish.

"We'll de-worm and flea-dip
Your mangy mutt Nevins!"

S.L.O.W. picked up Nevins and gave him a bath. When it plopped him down, he was clean and dry and had a little bow on his collar.

The Cat hopped off of S.L.O.W. as the Things waved good-bye and drove their machines right into the crate. Sally and I looked around in awe. The house was absolutely spotless! In fact, it was even better than it had been before.

> "Well, I guess that is that.
> The house is clean, and I'm glad.
> It's not as fun as making messes,
> But I guess it's not bad."

The Cat shut the crate with a flourish as the song ended. Outside we heard Mom step up to the door and then drop her keys.

The Cat didn't seem nervous. He dusted himself off and straightened his tie.

"All righty," he said. "Just one last thing to check . . ."

The Cat pulled out the phunometer and held it up to me and Sally. The needle went straight to the middle of the dial, where a green light glowed. The phunometer made a harmonious chord.

"Looks like everything's in balance!" the Cat said. To Sally he added, "And you've grown an inch."

The Cat smiled at us proudly. "I think you two have learned a lot today," he said. "You've learned to depend on one another."

Sally and I looked at each other. He was really leaving!

Sally was the first to speak. "This day has been . . . amazing. Thank you, Cat."

I put my arm around my sister. "For everything," I added.

The Cat took off his hat and gave us a little bow. For once, he was serious. "Conrad, Sally, *adieu.* So long, Nevins."

"Catch you later, Cat," Nevins said in a deep voice.

What?!? Sally and I stared at Nevins, stunned. He just barked and ran off. Behind us, the Cat and the Things slipped out the back door . . . just as the front door was opening. It was Mom!

Sally and I jumped into our seats by the window and put on our most innocent faces.

"All right, kids!" Mom said, flying through the door. "This place better not be a mess. I'm . . ."

Mom paused as she took in our beaming faces and the clean room. ". . . home," she concluded.

“Hi, Mom!” Sally and I cried.

Mom was looking around in disbelief. Secretly, I couldn’t blame her. But out loud, I asked, “What’s wrong?”

“Nothing,” Mom said. “That’s what’s so . . . odd. Wait a second,” she said, suddenly suspicious. “Where’s Nevins?”

As if on cue, Nevins ran into the room and jumped into my arms. His fur almost sparkled, it was so clean, and the bow on his collar didn’t hurt.

“I hope it’s okay,” I said. “We gave him a flea bath.”

Suddenly Mrs. Kwan sprang up off the couch, wide awake. “Ms. Walden!” she said. “Home so soon? The children were angels.”

Mom smiled. “They are, aren’t they? Thanks, Mrs. Kwan. I’ll walk you out.”

Mom opened the door and there, standing in the doorway, was Quinn! He looked terrible. He was completely caked with mud, and his hair was sticking out all over the place. Sally and I glanced at each other. I'm sure she was as curious as I was about what had happened to him after he'd fallen from the entryway.

But I've got to hand it to Quinn—he didn't give up. As we all stood there staring at him, he calmly said, "Hello, Joan."

My mom was aghast. "Lawrence, what happened to you?"

His eyes burning, Quinn pointed at me and Sally. "*They* happened to me! Your demon children! They've destroyed your entire *house*!"

It was only then that Quinn glanced around and saw how spotless the house was.

Sally smiled angelically. "Mommy, what is he talking about?"

Ha! I thought.

Quinn snarled and got right in Sally's face. "You know!" he said. "The house was alive, and the wall was made of paper, and I fell off a cliff! And the giant cat! The giant cat!"

I almost felt sorry for the guy. He sounded like a lunatic!

My mom was starting to think so, too. "Who?" she asked. "Lawrence, you're not making any sense."

I couldn't help myself. "Larry," I said, "you look terrible, and my mom thinks you're insane. That's what we in sales call a win-win."

Quinn quickly saw what was happening and tried his old strategy of sweet-talking my mom. "Joan," he said. "Joan . . . Joan. You're walking away from the opportunity of a lifetime. You know what kind of kid your son is. Who are you going to believe?"

Quinn gave my mom his sexiest look. It seemed to be working!

"You're right," my mom said.

My heart dropped.

"I do know what kind of kid Conrad is," my mom continued. "He can be irresponsible, he makes bad choices, and sometimes he makes me want to tear my hair out . . . but he's a good kid, and I believe in him."

Yes! I thought.

My mom pulled out the military school brochure and ripped it up. "Now I'd like you to leave," she said to Quinn.

Quinn fell to his knees in the doorway. "Joan," he said desperately. "Marry me!"

Mom stared at him for a moment—then shut the door in his face!

Sally and I ran to the window and watched as Quinn trudged down the walk back to his house. Nevins was sitting on the sidewalk, lapping at a pool of . . . I squinted. Was that purple water?

Sally gasped as Quinn reared back to kick Nevins, but Nevins bared his teeth. They were gigantic fangs! There must have been a little Cat magic left in that purple puddle.

Sally and I grinned at each other as we turned to help our mom get ready for the party.

So that's pretty much it. Believe it or not, that's the story of how the worst day ever became the best day ever. The party that night was a smashing success, by the way. All of Sally's friends came. She made up with them by baking a batch of cupcakes just for them. Even the Schweitzer kid showed up, sticking his hands in candles.

The Fish got a luxurious new tank. I caught a glimpse of him dancing to the music with Diver Dan.

Sally and I were hanging out together when Mom walked over, handing out cupcakes as she came.

"Your cupcakes are a huge hit, Sally," she said. "What did you put in them?"

Sally winked at me. "Mom, you can make cupcakes out of anything," she said.

I pretended to be shocked. "Are you telling me you can make cupcakes out of anything?"

"Anything," Sally said.

Sally and I giggled. Mom was clearly puzzled. "So what *did* you kids do today?"

Sally and I looked at each other knowingly.

Well?

What would *you* do if your mother asked *you*?